Dear Parents:

Congratulations! Your child is taking the first steps on an exciting journey. The destination? Independent reading!

STEP INTO READING® will help your child get there. The program offers five steps to reading success. Each step includes fun stories and colorful art or photographs. In addition to original fiction and books with favorite characters, there are Step into Reading Non-Fiction Readers, Phonics Readers and Boxed Sets, Sticker Readers, and Comic Readers—a complete literacy program with something to interest every child.

Learning to Read, Step by Step!

Ready to Read   Preschool–Kindergarten
• big type and easy words • rhyme and rhythm • picture clues
For children who know the alphabet and are eager to begin reading.

Reading with Help   Preschool–Grade 1
• basic vocabulary • short sentences • simple stories
For children who recognize familiar words and sound out new words with help.

Reading on Your Own   Grades 1–3
• engaging characters • easy-to-follow plots • popular topics
For children who are ready to read on their own.

Reading Paragraphs   Grades 2–3
• challenging vocabulary • short paragraphs • exciting stories
For newly independent readers who read simple sentences with confidence.

Ready for Chapters   Grades 2–4
• chapters • longer paragraphs • full-color art
For children who want to take the plunge into chapter books but still like colorful pictures.

STEP INTO READING® is designed to give every child a successful reading experience. The grade levels are only guides; children will progress through the steps at their own speed, developing confidence in their reading.

Remember, a lifetime love of reading starts with a single step!

For Jackson
—N.E.

Special thanks to Kelsey Howard,
Sherin Kwan, and Alex Wiltshire

All rights reserved. Published in the United States by Random House Children's Books, a division of Penguin Random House LLC, 1745 Broadway, New York, NY 10019, and in Canada by Penguin Random House Canada Limited, Toronto.

Step into Reading, Random House, and the Random House colophon are registered trademarks of Penguin Random House LLC.
Visit us on the Web!
StepIntoReading.com
rhcbooks.com
minecraft.net
Educators and librarians, for a variety of teaching tools, visit us at RHTeachersLibrarians.com

ISBN 978-0-593-37270-8 (trade)—ISBN 978-0-593-37271-5 (lib. bdg.)—ISBN 978-0-593-37272-2 (ebook)

Printed in the United States of America
10 9 8 7 6 5

MOBS IN THE OVERWORLD!

by Nick Eliopulos

illustrated by Alan Batson

Random House 🏠 New York

Birch threw a stick
high into the air.
It flew above the houses
of a Minecraft village.

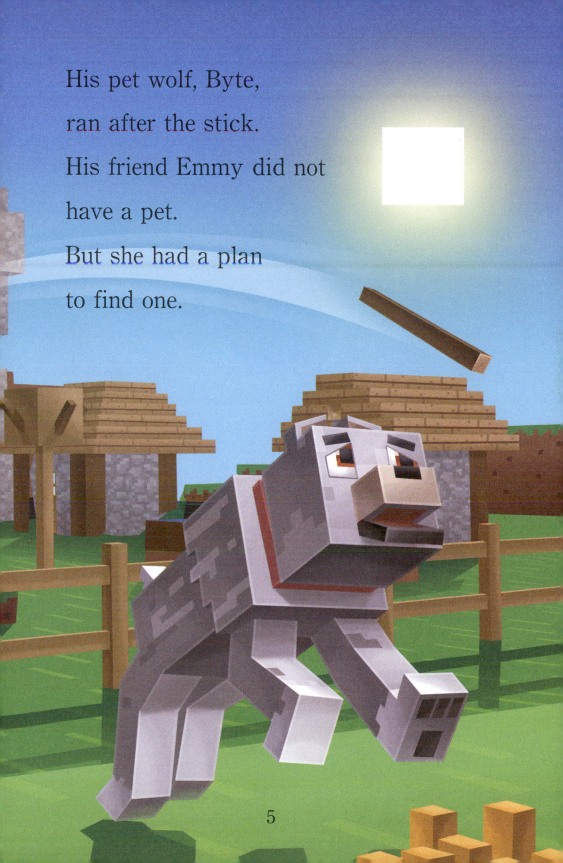

His pet wolf, Byte,
ran after the stick.
His friend Emmy did not
have a pet.
But she had a plan
to find one.

"Let's go exploring,"
said Emmy. "Somewhere
in the Overworld,
I will find my perfect pet."
Birch cheered.
Byte wagged his tail.
They liked exploring.

The creatures of Minecraft
were called mobs.
Emmy and Birch knew
that some mobs were peaceful
and some mobs were hostile.

There were many passive mobs in the village. Emmy saw sheep and chickens, a pig and a cow. "These mobs belong to the villagers," Birch said. Emmy agreed, so they went looking elsewhere for a mob to tame.

In a chilly forest called a taiga,

they found three rabbits.

Emmy thought they were very cute.

But she did not want

to take a bunny from its family.

Byte scared a fox away. GRRRR!

Birch spotted a bees' nest.

What luck!

Emmy could keep the bees,

and he could collect the honey.

"Wait!" cried Emmy.

Birch only wanted to knock
the nest out of the tree,
but he had forgotten
to build a campfire. Now the bees
were angry. BUZZZZZZ!

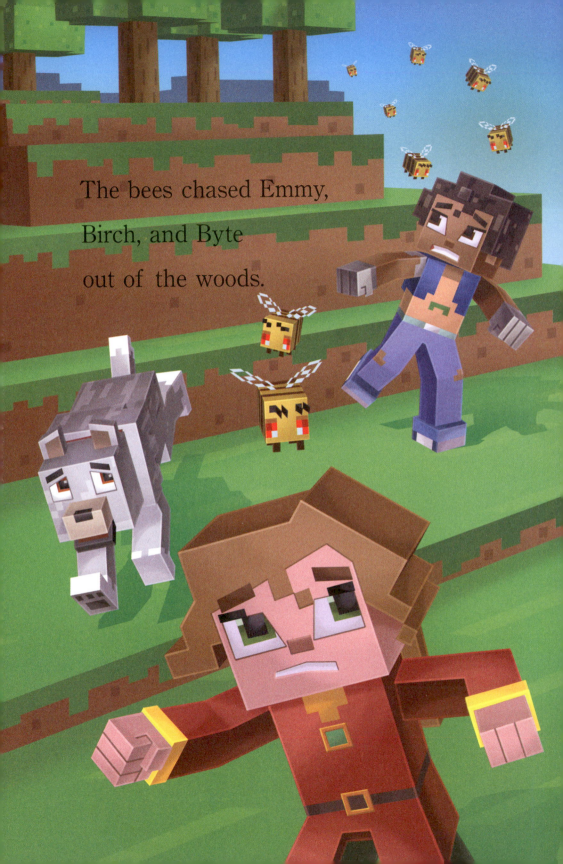

The bees chased Emmy,
Birch, and Byte
out of the woods.

"Bugs do not make good pets,"
said Emmy. "No bees, please.
And no spiders."

"And no silverfish!"
said Birch. "Yuck!"

13

The friends entered a cave.
It was a shortcut
through the mountain.
They saw some bats
sleeping high above.
But there were other mobs
living in the dark—hostile mobs!

Emmy and Birch saw movement
in the shadows.

A slime bounced.

A skeleton rode toward them
on a spider's back.

A zombie shuffled.

Byte leaped at the skeleton,
while Birch fought the spider.
Emmy used her bow
to send arrows flying
at the zombie and
the slime.

All the noise woke the bats!
They fluttered everywhere!
There was a light ahead.
Emmy and Birch fought
their way toward it.

They made it! Phew!

Outside the cavern,

the sun was still shining.

The friends soon found a jungle

full of bamboo,

where a baby panda

was rolling in the grass.

ACHOO!

The baby panda sneezed.

A slimeball flew

from the panda's nose

and almost hit Birch!

Maybe a panda was not

Emmy's perfect pet.

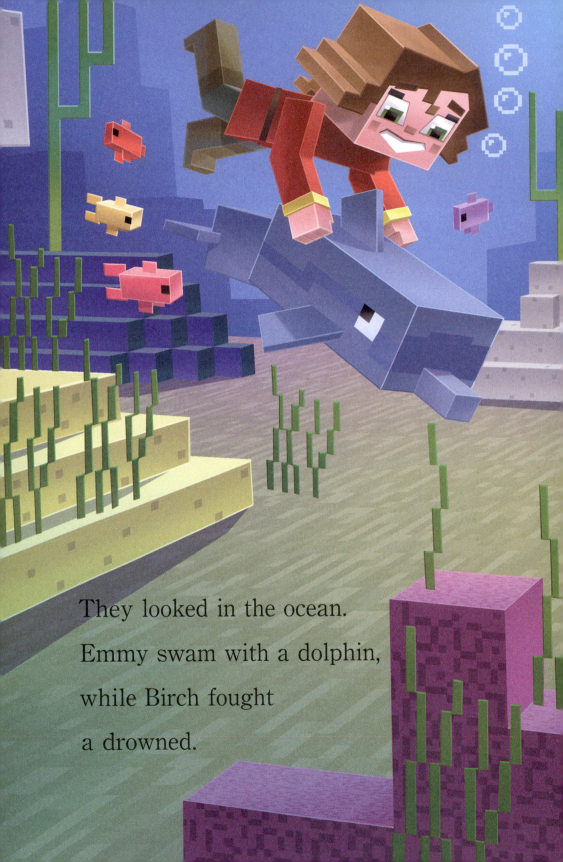

They looked in the ocean.
Emmy swam with a dolphin,
while Birch fought
a drowned.

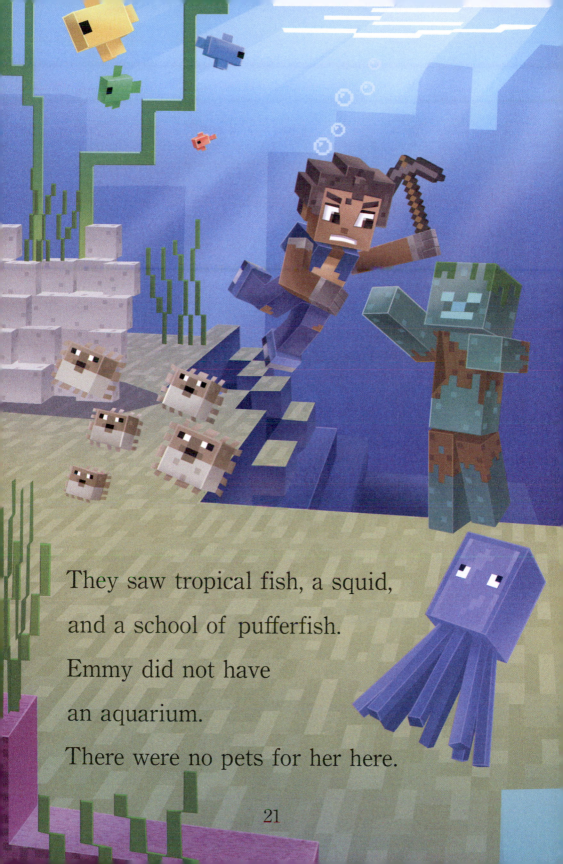

They saw tropical fish, a squid,
and a school of pufferfish.
Emmy did not have
an aquarium.
There were no pets for her here.

21

Next, they explored the snow and ice.

While Birch and Byte

fought with a frozen skeleton

called a stray,

Emmy searched for a pet.

She saw a polar bear cub
that was adorable—
but the mama bear growled
when Emmy got too close! GRRRR!
Emmy decided that a polar bear cub
would not want to be tamed.

Finally, after much exploring,
they came to a swamp.
Byte barked loudly
and pointed with his nose.

"It's a cat!" said Birch.
"Follow it," said Emmy.

But the black cat belonged

to a wicked witch.

She giggled and threw colorful potions.

Emmy, Birch, and Byte

ran away as fast as they could.

Some potions could be harmful.

They ran all the way
out of the swamp.
They did not hear
the HISS of a creeper
until it was too late!

The hostile mob exploded!

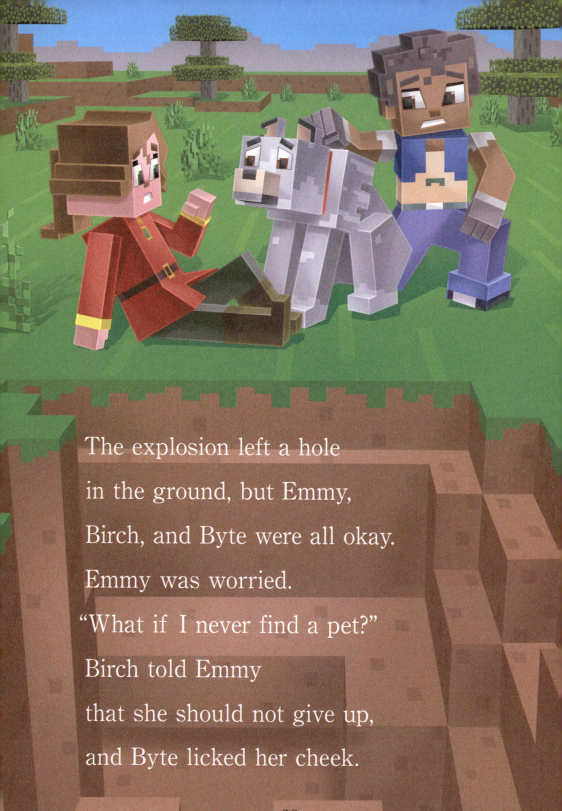

The explosion left a hole
in the ground, but Emmy,
Birch, and Byte were all okay.
Emmy was worried.
"What if I never find a pet?"
Birch told Emmy
that she should not give up,
and Byte licked her cheek.

Suddenly, they realized
there was a horse nearby,
standing in the grass
of the plains.
It was the most beautiful mob
Emmy had ever seen.

Birch crafted a lead.

He made it with string

from a spider and the slimeball

from the baby panda sneeze.

Emmy walked toward the horse.

Her movements were slow and quiet.

Emmy took the lead from Birch

while he gave the horse an apple.

"I will name her Ink," said Emmy.

Birch pulled a saddle

out of his inventory.

"You'll need this."

Emmy saddled Ink and climbed on.

Emmy galloped home on Ink's back.
Birch and Byte ran alongside them.
Their quest into the world of mobs
to find a pet had been a success.

MINECRAFT